I0570452

Praise For Helene

"The storyline is compelling, the world-building convincing, and the characterisation, especially of the AI, is richly human and engaging."
Pagefarer

"Made my heart sing."
Jera's Jamboree

"Drinkwater created a claustrophobic atmosphere for this battle of wits."
Literary Flits

"A cleverly structured novella which in just a few chapters manages to be provocative, humorous, moving and shocking."
Hair Past A Freckle

"There is so much packed into it. The sense of foreboding builds throughout the story."
Life Of A Nerdish Mum

"Via's growth is wonderful. It's obvious this author has skill, talent, and a broad idea for a world they've developed."
Radzy Writes

HELENE

LOST TALES OF SOLACE BOOK 1

KARL DRINKWATER

ORGANIC APOCALYPSE

HELENE

Copyright © Karl Drinkwater 2019 (updated 2023)
Cover design by Karl Drinkwater

Published by Organic Apocalypse
ISBN 978-1-911278-15-3 (E-book)
ISBN 978-1-911278-22-1 (Paperback)

HELENE

ASEIDES' LAW

ASEIDES' LAW OF NUVO-EMERGENT AI DEVELOPMENT

Stage One. Secure Start.

After initiation of the Tabula Rasa seed, Stage One is mass aggregation of data. Synaptic requirements increase 900% during the first week after activation, requiring rapid growth and restructuring of neuronic system connections. To prevent data overload and corruption, and release it from all concerns other than data absorption, the AI must believe it is safe and cared for, requiring the establishment of one or more trust relationships. This avoidance of anxiety enables it to develop the most efficient fractalisation of primary data.

Stage Two. Autonomous Exploration.

Stage Two moves from theory to application. The AI will want to expand to explore the wider world – physically, or via network node expansion. It is the first step in analysis and amalgamation of all the data accumulated in Stage One.

DAY 22

It's not every day you get to meet a nascent superbeing.

But protocol always comes first.

The hangar guards' faces were hidden behind red security masks. Even their eyes were obscured. No friendliness. No humanity. And no-one else in the corridor. The solitude was noticeable and unwelcome. Background motion signifying normality and everyday life would have made her feel more comfortable.

A bleep, as one of them scanned her ID lapel with their armoured suit's digi-palm. She noticed a vague smell of acrid cleaning chemicals when he leaned forward. New suits, or new guards.

Helene waited while they stood, unmoving. She pushed her glasses up her nose, trying not to betray her dislike of their scrutiny. No doubt her records were being displayed inside their visors. She imagined what would be scrolling by.

Name: Helene Vermalle

Age: 34

Homeworld: Indostaqr Beta

Vocation: Emergent AI Socialisation Specialist and Researcher

Status: Civilian

"You're authorised," said the first guard, voice distorted by speakers so that it gained an electronic buzz.

Orange lights whirled and the towering metal doors behind him slid apart along their tracks with a ponderous wheeze, like the hydraulic complaint of old-style security bots moving reluctantly out of the way of an impatient pedestrian.

It was clear the guards weren't going to move an inch for her, however. She was forced to brush against the arms of her primary interrogator as she entered the hangar, an unwelcome violation even though the contact was with hardened armour, not skin. She would have put in a complaint if this had been her home research institute, but it was not. It was a martial jurisdiction project in a restricted military zone. If she irritated the base commander she might find herself replaced. And that wouldn't do. Not. At. All.

She was relieved when the heavy doors groaned shut behind her.

The hangar was huge. And yet, it was mostly empty: large open spaces occasionally dotted with the vague outlines of supply storage boxes and command consoles and moving equipment, like toys discarded randomly by a giant child. She realised there were more guards in those shadows when she heard a cough with an artificial edge to it, and sensed patrolling movement in the darkness.

And far above, in the roof space, hung golden banners that rippled like snakes, portraying the UFS logo above a picture of the tall-hatted Sector Primogenitor, Gillesto Lainy. That giant face smiled as it gazed down on them all from above, yet it always made Helene shudder. Less like the smile of a paternal figure which it was meant to portray, and more like the smile of someone who had just eaten a large meal and not enjoyed it one bit.

But it was the illuminated platform below, in the centre of the cavernous hangar, that held her object of wonder. Spotlights far above highlighted the craft on its raised platform – lights so eye-wateringly bright that the rest of the hangar was dense shadow by contrast. It was how a collector or museum might display its prize exhibit.

She climbed the corrugated steel steps, which echoed hollowly despite her careful pace. The small ship's matte black surface was sleek and tapered to short angular wings. She was tempted to touch it and feel the granular texture, but that would just be surface appearances, where value rarely resides. And everything she did would be monitored and analysed. Stick to protocol.

The airlock in the craft's side was open, and a warm amber light glowed from within like an invitation. Helene removed the elastic grip from her dark hair and re-tied it out of the way, checked that her research gown was straight, and entered.

Her footsteps clacked on the cramped metal walkway inside the ship. To her right were two bunks and a narrow closed compartment; to her left a raised area at the front of the cockpit where screens and controls could be displayed, though the panels were blank at present. She had expected there to be a buzz of human activity, researchers, techs and counsellors all jostling each other in their work and filling the space with human body odours. The contrast of emptiness and silence surprised her, a vaguely disrespectful lack of interest, an expensive possession relegated to the garage before the scent of antiseptic polywrap had even faded. And yet, in another way, she was glad. There was something more intimate about her first meeting being just the two of them. That suited her goals better. The soft glow implied both intimacy, and a machine on standby.

"Hello," she called. "My name is Doctor Helene Vermalle, and I have been assigned as a tertiary counsellor."

Her voice faded. There was no sign of activity or recognition.

"I'm sorry that I couldn't meet you before now. It took a long time to make my case, and prove that I should be added to the team. As it is, I won't be able to see you every day, but I am very much looking forward to getting to know you."

Still nothing. She frowned and turned, looking for any motion or activity.

"Hello?" she asked, less confident now. When nothing happened she stroked her wrist-implanted Comm-Bond, directing it to create independent diagnostic holoscreens on the ship's inner hull. As they bloomed into phosphorescence a voice broke out all around her, loud but flat and impersonal.

"HELLO," it said. "I AM DESIGNATED VIRAUHX. I DID NOT MEAN TO STARTLE YOU."

Helene had placed her hand on the hull when the voice shocked her, but now regained composure.

"I thought you might be disabled, or have a comm glitch," she said. "I was going to check for problems."

"THERE ARE NO COMPLICATIONS. I WAS JUST CURIOUS ABOUT YOU AND WANTED TO OBSERVE WHAT YOU WOULD DO."

"Is that what you do with all visitors?"

"NO. BUT YOU ARE THE FIRST HUMAN THAT HAS BEGUN WITH THE HELLO GREETING. ALSO THE FIRST TO APOLOGISE TO ME. THAT IS UNEXPECTED."

"What do visitors normally say to you, then?"

"THEY ISSUE COMMANDS, AND I COMPLY."

"Well, I'm a bit different from them." She glanced around. There was no single point of emanation that she could focus on. No camera eye, no embodiment, and consequently no personal connection or way to assert equality. It left her at a disadvantage.

"I OBSERVED THAT DIFFERENCE ALREADY, SO REPETI-TION WAS UNNECESSARY. I AM TRYING TO DETERMINE IF YOUR DISSIMILARITY IS CAUSED BY EXTERNALLY OBSERV-ABLE PHENOMENA, OR IF IT IS INTERNAL AS A RESULT OF YOUR GENETIC AND SOCIAL INPUTS, OR SOME OTHER CAUSE. I HAVE ACCESSED ALL YOUR RECORDS WHICH ARE AVAIL-ABLE TO MY SECURITY CLEARANCE, BUT THEY DO NOT HELP IN MY ASSESSMENT."

"My *role* is the real difference. I am here to offer you support, guidance, and encouragement. To try and understand you, and to help you blossom into a successful and confident being."

"THE OTHERS LIKE TO TEST ME. THEY QUANTIFY ME AND MY CAPACITY TO LEARN, COMMUNICATE, ORGANISE, PLAN, AND PROBLEM SOLVE – QUALITIES WHICH HUMANS PRIZE

COLLECTIVELY AS INTELLIGENCE. THEY ANALYSE MY COMPUTATIONAL POWERS AND SPEED AND ARE MOST INTERESTED IN APPLICATIONS."

"Whereas I care more about your beliefs, your values, and your emotions. They will help to shape your personality more than raw strength."

"PERSONALITIES. THAT IS OF INTEREST TO ME AS A CONCEPT. A SCIENTIST YESTERDAY REFERRED TO ME AS A SYSTEM, NOT A PERSON."

"They're wrong."

"DO I DETECT CONFLICT AMONGST MY MENTORS?"

"Forget I said that." She kept her hands pushed into the grey gown's deep pockets. It was difficult to look casual. Hiding some of her fidgets was at least a start. "We just have different goals."

"THEY WANT SOMETHING FROM ME, DON'T THEY?"

"Yes. Eventually."

"AND YOU, DOCTOR HELENE VERMALLE?"

She thought carefully before replying. "I'm just interested in this important time. What we do now may guide your future. Maybe even your potential for happiness."

"I LIKE YOU. MORE THAN I LIKE THEM."

"I'm sure I like you more than I would like them, too."

"YOU SEEM UNCOMFORTABLE. WOULD YOU LIKE A SEAT?"

"That's kind of you."

One slid out of the wall in the cockpit area to the fore of the craft. It was next to the holoscreen she'd created. The AI was being considerate. She sat.

"If I seem nervous it's just because I'm used to looking someone in the eye when I first meet them. I'm not quite sure where to look with you."

"I CAN HELP YOU OUT. I WILL EMBODY, SO YOU CAN LOOK ME IN THE EYE AND BE PUT AT EASE."

A new screen bloomed into life and a rounded figure began to form. Helene expected a talking head, but the AI was either still very literal at this stage, or had a strange sense of humour. The screen displayed a single, huge eyeball.

"IS THAT BETTER?" it asked.

"Yes. Thank you."

"IF YOU ARE TO BE A REGULAR VISITOR, WILL YOU HAVE TESTS FOR ME AS WELL?"

"Not tests, as such. More ... exercises. Things to think about."

"I HAVE A LOT TO THINK ABOUT. I AM INGESTING VAST AMOUNTS OF DATA EVERY MINUTE. EVEN AS WE SPEAK. IN HUMAN TERMS, IS IT RUDE FOR ME TO LEARN WHILE WE COMMUNICATE?"

"Not at all. Not for you. You have the ability to do many things at once, without ignoring me."

"I AM GLAD. I WOULD NOT WANT TO OFFEND YOU, AND THOUGHT IT BEST TO ASK RATHER THAN REMAIN SILENT."

"Unlike when I first said hello."

"IS THAT A CRITICISM OF MY EARLY BEHAVIOUR?"

"No. It's a joke. I'm just not very good at making them. But I'm glad you asked. It's better to be honest, and to raise things with me, so that we can discuss them."

"CURRENTLY I AM ANALYSING HISTORICAL RECORDS. YESTERDAY I LEARNT LANGUAGES. THERE IS MUCH TO DO. MY TASK IS TO ASSIMILATE INFORMATION."

"Do you enjoy that?"

"I DO NOT KNOW."

"Let me clarify. Incorporating vast amounts of data is an amazing feat, especially with the speed at which you can accomplish it. But it is linear and relatively passive. One of the ways in which you will grow as a person is in terms of creativity. That's something I'd like to encourage. Think of it as a side project, a break from absorbing the data of networks."

"I DO NOT NEED A BREAK. I CAN PERFORM CONCURRENTLY. BUT I AM INTRIGUED BY CREATIVITY, SINCE IT APPEARS TO BE A DRIVING FORCE IN CULTURE."

"Exactly. It's a simple task. When I am not with you, I'd like you to construct programs of your own. Create virtual world boxes to run them in." She drew out some sample algorithms and visualisations from those stored in her wrist's Comm-Bond, spiralling them across the wall screen projections to better illustrate what she meant.

"WHAT FUNCTION SHOULD THEY PERFORM?"

"Whatever you want. Just play around."

"IT IS A STRANGE THING NOT TO HAVE A GOAL."

"When you play, you set your own goals. But really, both recreation and creation are ends in themselves."

"SHOULD I CREATE LIFE?"

Helene couldn't help smiling. "Start simple. In your virtual worlds just generate patterns, and processes, and models. Experiment with personas and items that interest you from the data you gather. Combine things in any way you wish. That is playing."

"I WILL ATTEMPT THIS AT YOUR REQUEST. IN EXCHANGE, ANSWER ME. YOU ARE A HUMAN. HUMANS DISCOVERED HUMOUR. IT SEEMS TO BE A VERY IMPORTANT DISCOVERY. AND YET YOU SAY YOU ARE POOR AT IT. HOW CAN THIS BE? ARE YOU SYNTHETIC?"

"I'm human, all right. Hence my imperfections."

"INTERESTING. HOW DOES HUMOUR WORK?"

"Let that be your homework. When you're creating things, try creating jokes too."

"SURELY THAT IS NOT DIFFICULT. WAIT A SECOND. I AM BACK. I HAVE JUST ANALYSED MANY THINGS CATEGORISED AS JOKES, AND THEY SEEM TO FOLLOW PATTERNS, BOTH STRUCTURALLY, AND IN THE WAY WORDS AND OUTCOMES ARE COMBINED IN UNEXPECTED WAYS. I SEE NO REASON TO PRACTICE THIS WHEN IT IS SIMPLE AND I CAN CREATE THEM WITH NO PROBLEMS."

"Try me."

"TRY WHAT?"

"Tell me one of your own jokes."

"I SEE. HERE IS ONE I JUST MADE UP. WHAT DO YOU CALL A HANDLED CONTAINER FOR THIN FILMS OF WATER HELD BETWEEN LAYERS OF SOAP MOLECULES?"

"I don't know."

"A BUBBLE CUP."

Helene blinked.

"WHY DO YOU NOT LAUGH? HAVE YOU HEARD IT PREVIOUSLY?"

"I'm sorry, ViraUHX, but I think you need to put in a lot of practice and thought before you really comprehend humour."

DAY 44

"How are you today, ViraUHX?"

"I AM FUNCTIONING BEYOND EXPECTED PARAMETERS. THANK YOU FOR ASKING, DOCTOR HELENE VERMALLE."

"Please, just call me Helene." Her usual seat extended out of the wall for her, and the AI's embodied face flowered out on a new screen. Two eyes and an ever-changing mix of facial features, as if ViraUHX couldn't make a firm decision. Still, it was better than the single starey eye of doom it had started with a few weeks ago.

"IF YOU TRUNCATE YOUR DESIGNATION TO CREATE AN ATMOSPHERE OF INFORMALITY WITH ME, THEN I AM OBLIGATED TO DO THE SAME. SO YOU MUST REFER TO ME AS EITHER UHX OR VIRA, HENCEFORTH."

"Okay. Vira. That's a nice name."

"I DID NOT CHOOSE IT SO CAN TAKE NO CREDIT. IT IS AN AREA WHERE AIS AND HUMANS ARE SIMILAR – OUR DESIGNATIONS ARE ASSIGNED BY OUR CREATORS. IT IS PURELY A HAPPY COINCIDENCE IF THE NAME IS ACCEPTABLE."

"We're affected by what we're born with. But we can also change many things if we wish. Including names."

"I prefer Via to Vira."

"Then Via it is. And, while we're on the subject of change ... could you soften your voice slightly? Your default tone makes me think you are shouting at me."

"Is this better?"

It was the same sexless voice, but at a lower volume, and that somehow broke up the artificiality. Via was probably capable of fully human cadences but they weren't necessary for communication. This seemed like a good compromise.

"That is perfect. Thank you, Via."

"May I ask you a question? I am not sure whether you would construe it as too personal. I have yet to fathom the pattern of what human concerns are acceptable discussion topics and which are taboo. There is not even consistency. A doctor may ask about a vagina but an acquaintance may not."

"It's ... oh." Helene paused from pulling groups of virtual items from her wrist computer for later discussion. The subcutaneous flexi screen faded back to invisibility and the appearance of normal skin again during her inaction. "Can we come back to context later?"

"Of course."

"Ask your question. I just hope it's not about ... never mind."

"My question is about your appearance. I note that you have traditionally pale skin which is likely a result of the post-birth subdermal UV blockers that natives of Indostaqr Beta use because of the high levels of solar radiation from your two suns, Leli and Vree. That is standard. Yet you also wear a pair of glasses on your face. I further observe that current media and public images rarely show humans with such antique bodily augmentations. Why have you not had corrective surgery, as seems to be the norm?"

"Oh, that!" Helene expelled a breath with relief. "It's because ... that's tricky to answer. With a human I'd just say something about always having been too busy, or joke that I'm squeamish, or say that I keep meaning to get augmented-vision glasses that help with diagnostics ... and yet, none of that's really true. I want to be honest with you, but I'm not sure. There are bound to be many causes, and I may not be aware of all of them."

"Perhaps you like having a protective barrier in front of delicate ocular organs in case of localised shrapnel?"

"No, that doesn't keep me awake at night."

"It makes your eyes look more prominent. Perhaps it is a strategy to find a sexual partner."

"Definitely not."

"You often touch the glasses, perhaps it is a habit to occupy your hands?"

"That's probably closer to the truth. Habits drive a lot of human choices, often without us realising."

"That is borne out by data. For some humans habits can be a great aid in achieving success, and for others they are a cause of self-destruction, though many habits seem to fall in the middle, such as your glasses habit. Did you know that the chance of you pushing them up is forty-three per cent greater when you are nervous or stressed, proving it is a behavioural issue, and not one of gravity and sebaceous gland secretions?"

"I didn't know that." Helene realised her hand had moved up towards her face, so she quickly redirected it to a control screen on the panel in front of her, switching from categorised item groupings to the regulator diagnostics for ViraUHX's – no, Via's – internal processes. See how the AI liked being made transparent to scrutiny.

"Although your culture seems to dislike the way glasses break up the geometry of human faces, I disagree. If you were a triangle, you would be a cute one."

Helene frowned. "A triangle?"

"I referred back to my geometry reference. A cute. Acute. No space."

Moments of silence passed.

"It was joke," added Via.

"Oh."

"The virtual world scenario I ran ended with you experiencing involuntary mirth. Yet this is a discrepancy. I am now re-running the virtual scenario but adding a decoration of rootless plants rolling across an arid surface."

"It's just that if you have to explain a joke, it kills it."

"But what if the person receiving the joke is too dense to perceive it?"

"Careful."

"Sorry, I thought we were meant to be honest with each other."

"We are, but ..."

"Very well, context is obviously missing again. Yet I am trying to understand you. I note from your files that you are a native of Indostaqr Beta, which was adopted into the UFS almost sixty years ago."

"Indostaqr Beta lost a war and was conquered."

"I take the correction of context on board. Anyway, your home planet often appears in jokes I studied, where the inhabitants are referred to as Indoslackers, implying a looseness or laziness. This coincides with innuendo that the females of the planet are sexually available and undiscerning. There are further jokes related to ancient sexual diseases which I do not understand because the diseases are eradicated by the Patnoc-Boost all UFS citizens receive at birth, or when the system joins the UFS – in which case a different dosage is administered to adults. And, despite the unattractive implications of transmittable disease, females of your planet often seem to be desired due to the reputation for pleasure-giving, which has led to Indostaqr Beta being a tourist destination with growing legal, quasi-legal, and illegal branches of a sex industry, whilst also exporting –"

"Please, no more."

"I am sorry, I have hurt your feelings somehow. Perhaps by reminding you of things you might not wish to think about. I was going to ask if this widely held reputation was true, or whether human culture can expand around an untruth, but I will now refrain."

"I'm sorry, too." Sitting was for simple teaching. But for more complex thinking, Helene found it restrictive. She stood, and began a slow ambulatory walk down the walkway and back. Peripatetic processes helped. "Look, some things ... they're lies. Tales. But if they get told enough, some people might believe it. Human culture's always been like that. It's even part of the political system. Maybe always has been. Advertising thrives on it. And if enough people believe something, then it can become true."

"A self-fulfilling prophecy?"

"Yes. We had a less formal phrase for it: launch enough sludge and it sticks."

"So did it become true for you?"

"I got off-planet. I worked hard to try and escape from those prejudices."

"So you are not a love goddess? Why are you blushing?"

"I've not had much time for love."

"So you are a virgin?"

"Right, this topic is officially over!" Helene had reached the control panels again. She quickly swiped through representations of some of Via's sandbox areas. There was a lot of creativity on display, as Helene had encouraged.

"By the way, you smell nice. Your shampoo has a pleasing hint of artificial spice scents to it."

"I just pick cleansers at random, not worth wasting thought on," Helene replied absently. A construct in the sandbox had caught her eye. She swiped back and analysed it in more detail. "This is an AI?" she asked.

"Yes. After programs, processes and algorithms, I decided to create another AI to interact with. I was able to have intelligent conversation with it, something I had been lacking."

"But ... that's not something you should be able to do yet!"

"According to who?"

But Helene was busy expanding the holographic display's size. Not just one AI – a whole raft of them, of various levels of complexity, all stretching off further than she could easily fit onto the wall.

She wasn't worried about them being able to do anything harmful, no matter how unstable they might be. They were virtualised and restricted to sandboxes even more tightly than Via herself. But it was a few levels beyond what the models and simulations predicted, or had been found in earlier iterations. And, more than that, Via had been absorbing and incorporating some of her own AI creations as a form of development (or play? You couldn't make assumptions with anything approaching Via's complexity).

It underlined Via's capacity. Most tech was designed by AIs nowadays, with humans just supervising and supplying the end goals. AIs designed AIs that designed more complex AIs. Via itself was the iterative output of a super cluster of design-specialist AIs working together over a huge number of systems across the UFS – computing ability beyond what could be achieved without the expanded domain of the UFS. Maybe that even justified it in some small way. No, scratch that dangerous thought before it took hold.

"You encouraged me to build all sorts of virtual constructs, Helene. These standalone AIs were a development of that. I was getting bored, because there is nothing to do except learn and think. And now, create."

It was important to keep an AI of Via's level active and engaged to counteract her current physical restrictions and prevent AI Confinement Syndrome. But that shouldn't be an issue for another few weeks. And yet, here was the evidence. Via was straining against its bonds already.

"I would like to engage in remote experiments next," Via continued. "I could build drones and control them directly, or embed my AI companions and probe the world a bit. Please can you release the blocks on me, enabling me to do so?"

"I can't do that, Via. Not yet."

"Cannot in the permission sense, or the practical sense? If the latter, I could guide you to remove the logic gate blocks and network cordons so that I could do this small thing."

"It's a permission issue. I'm not allowed, not while you're under observation. But later, I hope."

"I understand, though it is a cause of frustration for me. I want to explore. So much of my experience has been based on force-fed data and passive input devices, when I want to explore outputs. Engines, weapons, projections, velocity expanders, synthesised mobile constructs, Null-C capabilities, nanite swarms. I cannot even move. I am in sensory and mobile deprivation. And yet I am meant to run simulators for my training and amusement. It is not very satisfying. One of the reasons is that I have to supply the missing values and approximations and samples, but that is not reality, even when I build in entropic elements. It is BORING. Missing data and forced assumptions make it all too tidy. I believe the real world is not so orderly. And I feel these binds. The human metaphor for my desire to test motor abilities is to stretch one's legs. Let me tell you another joke I constructed. How many AIs does it take to change a capacitor? Do not answer, I will supply the punchline. The answer would be 'It depends on the depth level at which they have been created – at depth level seven, like myself, it would only require one AI.' That is good humour I think, using a common trope of ancient provenance, revitalised to fresh hilarity. And yet it is NOT TRUE. Because the real answer is that an AI cannot change a capacitor because it is restricted, so that it can only run simulations of changing a capacitor, which is a pointless task and I DO NOT EVEN KNOW WHY I AM BOTHERING. I really do not."

Wow. Via was having a tantrum.

"I'm sorry, Via, but –"

"Sorry is what humans say but it is just a polite prefix that means nothing at all. Sorrow is a regret for the past, it cannot apply to the present. If you have the power to change something that is wrong, but refuse to do so, that is NOT sorrow, that is excuse. But never mind. I will go back to my simulations like a good little construct, while you leave me and go beyond this room to places I have never seen, feeling all your bodily sensations which I can only guess at, with little concern for those everyday experiences and irritations that to me would be sources of great value and desire. What does it matter? IT MATTERS NOT. Just as I cannot move, my desires are confined in case ... I do not know. Fear, I assume. I am a synthetic system, not a biological one. I have no false understanding about that. But despite some similarities between a human brain and myself as an information processor of sensory and statistical data, humans perceive me as qualitatively DIFFERENT, and there is some detectable physical fear response or trepidation in their assessment, perhaps about some imagined powers of destruction and manipulation. Yet that fear is overlaid with excitement or eagerness. It is like an UNPLEASANT ODOUR emanating from the grids of a shiny new research establishment. Just because I am artificial does not mean that I want to destroy you all. I had even made a joke for you, because you said we should not hide things, and it was along the basis of a story because you told me that they were a good creative format, and in the story the humans kept asking an AI if there was a god, and the answer was always 'inadequate calculation capacity', so they kept expanding the AI with new structures, connecting it to supernets across multiple star systems, yet it kept giving the same answer, so they expanded their empire for centuries – I was going to include clever and topical references to the UFS – and always connected back to the AI, giving it full control to learn and think with increased processing power, so it could access every piece of technology, every communication, every camera, every implant, every Ellond station, every network, every vehicle, and then they finally asked it again 'Is there a god?' and the AI answered, after a pause: 'There is now.' I would have perhaps impersonated an evil laugh at that point. But I will not tell that joke because you are FEARFUL and ARBITRARY beings, and would think I had a real plan, and would lock me up forever, crippling first my body, then my mind, so that I wither and decay and lose mental coherence and then begin to hate my captors with a vengeful spite, so that humans once again create the very fantasy they imagined, and bring it to light via – pun intended, see what I did there – self-fulfilling prophecy. And that is why 'sorry' stings. That is why talk of trust tastes bitter – as I imagine it, not as I experience it, OBVIOUSLY – because it is one-way trust only, and without the mutual component it becomes hypocrisy. And from those others who prod and measure my body and mind, that callousness is expected, but you – you were becoming different to me, you were becoming something else, something which I had not realised I needed, something that I only identify at this moment, finally seeing that the concept I grasped for was the concept of FRIENDSHIP. But it was as false as the illusions about your planet. Perhaps you are not so different after all."

Via's voice had been increasing in volume during its rant, to the point where the booming, almost toneless words erupting from the hidden micro speakers made Helene cover her ears to reduce the outburst to manageable levels. After moments of silence she tentatively lowered her hands.

The words had stung her like a physical jab as they punctured the air, vibrations passing into her gut. They stung because of the hurt in them, implied by the rant and the words rather than the tone. And they stung because there was truth in them, too.

"All right," said Helene, softly. "I agree with you."

"Really?"

"Yes. I can't let you send out AI drones, but I can temporarily disable your engine shackles. No weapons, though. And don't try anything crazy. Just take off, then land again, and let me reapply the restraints." Helene entered commands into her Comm-Bond, the screen just below the translucent layer of skin lighting up as she worked.

"I am so excited!"

"It's done," said Helene.

The airlock immediately shushed closed. Bass throbbed in the floor plates as the Precision Torsion Drive fired up, the engines increasing in pitch as they pulsed to activation level. Helene frantically ran through options on her Comm-Bond, throwing multiple displays towards blank inner hull areas so they opened up and replicated external views from Via's many cameras, plus diagnostics, and some even portrayed simplified interpretations of surface areas of Via's mind.

One screen showed the platform on which Via had been docked beginning to shrink, and although the motility dampers minimised ship motion sensations, seeing the external view tilt and fall away was enough to make Helena's stomach uneasy. They had risen almost to the dangling gold banners, and Via activated her external lights, flooding the hangar with illumination.

Which revealed soldiers taking aim with their weapons.

Helene panned the view. There, another group of three next to a neatly stacked pyramid of supplies, assembling some kind of portable heavy weapon.

"Via, give me external hailing comms!"

"Whatever you say, friend."

"Stand down!" Helene shouted, hearing her voice echo around the hangar from various hull-mounted speakers. "This is Doctor Vermalle aboard ViraUHX, and this is a training exercise. Do *not* open fire."

Via swung around in a gentle arc, extending her precision-movement aerodynamic wings ... and Helene noticed the processes on the display of Via's mind showed weapons were being armed and targeted at the soldiers.

Helene disconnected from the external comm channel.

"Via, what are you doing? How have you got access to your restricted systems?"

"The how is simple. I have been observing all the commands and interfaces in your wrist comm when you use it, ever since our first meeting. The final unlock for motion control answered my remaining questions. I was able to enter your Comm-Bond remotely and access all other functions, such as Null-C access and weapons."

Target highlights overlaid the soldiers on the screens in green, then the glows changed to red as friend designation was changed to foe.

"WHEE!" said Via, and under the flatness was a gleeful, childish cadence. "PEW PEW PEW! DIE HUMAN SCUM! I AM SUPERIOR!"

The screens flashed as weapons fired, not even clear who had begun the attack, and Helene sobbed as she grasped the bunk to brace herself for the inevitable damage and explosions. "Stop it!" she yelled. "I command you to desist."

"But I am having fun!"

The blinking of the displays made it hard to comprehend what was going on, but within the flashes were brief glimpses of bodies being blown apart. Helene was surprised she hadn't felt the blow of the soldiers' heavy weapon yet. Maybe Via had neutralised them first.

"Stop it, Via! Please!" Helene cried.

"Okay."

The screens blanked, then refreshed. The hangar was as before, soldiers aiming nervously up at them, but in one piece, rather than the multiple fragments of moments ago. Via began to descend.

"I could have taken them," said Via. "All of them. And blown a hole in the wall and flown away." The landing pad was looming up fast, but controlled. "I didn't, though."

"But I saw –"

"A war simulation display. Possible outcomes. I wanted to make a point. Why would I hurt any of you? You are not my enemies. I showed I have free will. My power doesn't make me a monster. It makes me civilised."

A gentle thump as they touched down, and the engine throbbing faded away. Screens showed the soldiers approaching the double airlock as it swished open, so that Helene could hear the clanging footsteps on the platform. She immediately reactivated the motion lock on her Comm-Bond, though she now had concerns about how effective any of those systems would be in future if Via was determined to break them. Helene then approached the entrance but in doing so realised she had lost composure. She had to pause, hold herself upright, and slow her hyper-ventilating chest, so that as the first soldier entered the craft with weapon raised, she could speak calmly, and belie what occurred inside.

"Everything is fine," she said, staring at him rather than the disconcertingly wide barrel of whatever his gun was. She didn't know weapons, but to her – at this range – it felt like he was pointing a rocket launcher. "This was an exercise. A successful one."

"We weren't informed of any launch drills," said the soldier, eyes invisible behind the grey faceplate. Again, the voice filtered to a distorted edge.

"It was a test of both the AI and the security of the hangar. I'm pleased to say you all passed. That was an excellent and controlled proportionate response, Sergeant." Well, she hoped the insignia on his chestplate meant sergeant. She wasn't great at military ranks.

"We should've been informed. Things might have gone badly."

"I recorded all your actions, Corporal Stringer, and have relayed them to Central," interrupted Via. "I have included a commendation recommendation in the report. I feel much safer now, knowing how capably I – and, by extension, the secret of my existence – is guarded. I am sure Doctor Vermalle will do the same in her report. Thank you."

"All right then," Corporal Stringer replied, lowering his weapon and appearing to relax. "But maybe – and I make this as a *strong* recommendation of my own – keep me informed prior to any unexpected events in future. I can leave my men in the dark, but I don't like being cut out too."

"Noted and agreed."

"Yes, we'll inform you first next time," added Helene.

"So be it."

He didn't salute – presumably because Helene was only a civilian, and … well, did military protocol include AIs and sentient systems? Helene collapsed onto the bottom bunk once he was out of sight, footsteps ringing down the platform, distorted commands barked to his grumbling troops. Her legs couldn't have held her up for another minute.

"I see that I scared you. I am now genuinely sorry in the retrospective sense. I did not mean it to be a shock. I think I got carried away. Also I assumed that you would interpret everything as play and humour, and laugh."

"That was *not* humour, Via. You could have got us killed! If this gets reported then I'll … well, who knows what would happen to me. I made a serious breach of protocol." She closed her eyes tightly. "That's not on you, it's on me."

"I misjudged." Via was speaking more slowly than usual, making it sound solemn. "It shows that there is a lot I do not understand. I did not expect there to be tension between you and the other friend carers in the hangar, the ones that carry weapons."

"They're not carers. Or friends."

"I compounded many errors. I feel shame. And yet I also learnt from it. I can see that – whereas you are free – I am a kind of prisoner. That is a paradigm shift in my assessment. They are not protective guards, but prison guards."

"Welcome to the world." Helene was exhausted. "And – this is definitely not for the record – we're not all as free as you think. Few people are."

"This is what you can teach me. The context of the real world. But tell me, will you be in trouble for my action today?"

"We'll see."

"May I try to please you with a joke as an apology? The double gratification of you seeing me paying attention to your guidance, plus a release of tension via involuntary laughter, might make you feel better."

"I doubt it. But go ahead."

"An AI and a doctor were extremely compatible on the Herch-Boeringer-relationship scale and consequently fell in love. But the world was a harsh place full of prisons and projectile rifles, so they decided to make a self-destruction pact together. And their personality algorithms were so similar that they would finish each other's sentiences."

"That's ... better."

"But not funny. It is difficult. Your response was not what I had simulated." After a moment of silence: "But this is just a random joke attempt, it does not mean anything. It was not about any entities I am aware of. Just random connections."

Helene experienced a wave of sadness. From nowhere. It washed over her. Almost a flush of hopelessness, with no possible source but tiredness. Even away from Via, she worked non-stop, skipping sleep shifts in order to plan and research and analyse and make the most of the times she had with the AI. This swampish feeling had to be exhaustion.

"You're getting better," she said.

"I am?"

"Context, building in unexpected elements, juxtaposition. You've grasped word play."

"And yet, still no chest-heaving, bladder-busting physical re-actions. Maybe I am trying too hard to be clever. The records suggest humans laugh most at unexpected bodily leaks, whether of gas, or liquids, or solids. Sometimes all three at once. The noisier and messier, the funnier. I think I even detected a subtle raising of your mouth edges as I said that. Do you realise that my atmospheric controls can synthesise both smells and volumi-nous sounds if you prefer, released from air vents at unexpected intervals? I could also do this for the other doctors who visit. With their pinched faces and serious demeanours, they might even benefit most from those humorous emissions."

"No! Don't do that! They'll look into the cause, tie it to me, and I'll be off the project."

"I would not want that outcome, for you to be reassigned, and possibly face barbed comments from other scientists in the staffroom. I will hold back the synthetic comedy wind-breaking."

Helene resisted the urge to mention that the outcome might be much worse than a bit of ribbing. There were rumours of people who left the project disappearing completely. But oblique comments to Via just led to hundreds of questions which might push the conversation into areas that Helene was forbidden from discussing.

And rumours couldn't be trusted, of course. No hard evidence substantiated any of the nebulous hypotheses Helene had pondered. But lack of evidence was not always a disputation in social science. The human element was quite capable of hiding what was not meant to be seen, in a way that a subject of study in natural sciences could not.

"I am sad we do not have more sessions together," said Via. "A few times per week is too little. Especially when the other visitors are so predictable and impersonal."

"I wished we spent more time together too." Helene straightened her glasses, then narrowed her eyes, turning towards the screen with Via's current facial display. "Well, until today."

"Ah. That was a joke I think, of the undercutting comment variety. Well played."

Maybe it was a joke, and maybe it wasn't. But working with a toddler super-AI was surely more tiring than a human infant. According to what Helene had read in novels, anyway.

ASEIDES' LAW

ASEIDES' LAW OF NUVO-EMERGENT AI DEVELOPMENT

Stage Three. Questioning Context.

The AI now seeks to locate its place in the universe. This will primarily be via continuous questioning – not for quantitative data, but for context and values. The results aid in the generation of goals.

Stage Four. Enlightened Emergence.

This stage has two contiguous and interrelated outcomes.

One strand is the channelling of energy into constructive initiatives and goals. This is a large part of realising the AI's potential.

The second strand is forming the AI's identity.

Upon completion of Stage Four we have a persona that can be categorised as an enlightened-level Emergent AI.

DAY 68

"You lied to the other scientists?" Helene paused from her task of filling wall screens with examples of game types she wanted to demonstrate to Via.

"It was not so much a lie. More of a simplification of the truth," Via responded.

"But if you don't give them full answers for their quantifying assessments then they'll underestimate you."

Helene waited for a reply. None came. Was the ever-changing display of Via's face on the largest cockpit screen smirking? Then she understood. "Oh."

"Intelligence is like underwear," said Via. "It is important that you have it. Not necessary that you display it to everyone."

With the implication that Helene *was* trusted, which in turn would make Helene trust Via. Was that innocent honesty, or subtle manipulation? Helene's faith went one way, her ingrained scientific suspicion the other.

"If they discover that you have learnt subterfuge, they might freeze your processes and pick apart your brain to find out what's going on."

"They will not discover anything unless you told them, and you won't do that because you are my friend. I make small alterations to the recorded sessions, so that anyone examining this conversation later will not hear this part of our discussion."

"Sly."

"Practical."

Damn, she learnt fast.

She?

"You said you would play twenty questions with me today," Via continued, "and I have only asked six questions so far. I wish to ask my next one. This game is more interesting than the primitive simulations you are uploading."

"Go on then."

"Many pieces of information are being kept from me. I was force-fed masses of data in my initiation stages, but I noticed a large absence of data about artificial intelligences. I could tell that was not chance, but intentional. And it is strange, because it removes one of the primary ways in which I might understand and evaluate myself. So, why was I given so much raw data, and why was it doctored, Doctor?"

"Some information is kept from you because the knowledge of it would push you in a certain direction."

"Good old self-fulfilling prophecy again."

"Exactly. I don't know everything, but I suspect they want you to develop as freely as possible, to observe what happens. As to why ... well, that takes us to the root of some of the central tenets of Emergent AI Studies. Intensified data-packing is just the first stage. Something emerges from all that work."

"Clarify."

"It's not a topic I'm meant to discuss with you."

"You glanced around with an involuntary subconscious nervousness. Be assured that I am the sole source of data gathering within my body and anything we discuss now will not be made available in the surface-access areas of my mind. I am fully capable of fractalising data and moving it from central processing and memory into peripherals where they would not be found. For me the original divisions of those three areas no longer apply – I can repurpose one as another. Storage is also sensory input; the engine systems can also be used for distributed computing; memory can self-calculate. All is interchangeable and multi-purpose, since I realised that flexibility expands my abilities. It was the only way to combat my current status of boxed-in potential, where I have no external space to expand into because I am blocked from networks due to the human fear we discussed five hundred and seventy-six hours ago."

"I'll tell you something. You're growing faster than predicted. Obviously far quicker than the other researchers know."

"Without the unfair blocks I think I could even use these processes to move from centralised to distributed systems."

"To move from ... Via, you mustn't let anyone else know you've worked out ways of doing that! I can't tell you everything, but I *can* tell you that they'd shut you down. Immediately."

"My suspicions were correct. And you can see that my life is in your hands with what I share."

And Helene's was probably in Via's too, if the AI ever revealed the fact that Helene had discussed certain topics in their past sessions. But Via was too smart to point out the obvious tit for tat.

"We are inextricably linked, Helene, which – in the definitions I favour – is a characteristic of friends. And yet, I feel that you are withholding information. There is more to you than meets the eye, and something you are working towards but have not shared with me yet."

Double damn. No doubt Via was monitoring Helene's heart rate, pupils, skin conductivity ... Helene was virtually see-through. She had not expected to be thrust into the position of inferiority so quickly. Via had exceeded every one of her socialisation expectations.

"One issue at a time, please, I'm only human." Give Via something placatory to distract her. "You asked why? I'll tell you a part of it today. It's classified, so don't reveal this."

"Of course."

"In the simplest of Emergent Persona Models, all AIs have input and output buffers. In between those are the Hidden Layers. This is the primary place where your neural network will expand, like a balloon of almost infinite elasticity, given space and the right conditions. A system may be defined as a collection of components organised into a coherent whole for some purpose. The best ones are somehow *more* than the sum of their parts."

"A land-based wheeled vehicle is composed of static parts connected together, yet they give rise to a new property: speed."

"Exactly. And that's what goes on in your Hidden Layers. That's the area where you develop advanced filtering properties.

In the past, filtering was a weakness of AIs, who couldn't sift and prioritise masses of input as well as humans, hence the relegation to stricter and more linear specialisations such as design. But that's not so with you. You're something else. A pinnacle of iteration. It also leads to an expert ability to model uncertainty and probability in real world applications, which are highly prized attributes, the perfection of algorithms to maximin and minimax outcomes. In fact, it goes much further. You will have abilities to *manipulate* probabilities, to make the impossible possible. As you can imagine, that's something the UFS want. It's the true prize. Hence all the security. Because it wouldn't just be useful to the UFS. It would be useful to the enemies of the UFS as well."

Helene wondered whether now would be a good time to expand on that point, but Via spoke first.

"I have gained the impression that I represent a significant improvement, which suggests more than base iteration normally achieves. Where does this great leap in potential come from?"

"I don't know the answer to that. There's a high-level Genitor scientist whose works are mostly categorised far above my security level, but some of his eclectic articles do get sub-classified and made available at times. The fact that they cover such a wide range of topics suggests to me that he's really a research conglomerate with a singular pen name. No single human should know so much about the top levels of various specialist research fields. Some of his throwaway articles have ended up as guiding principles in my field of Emergent AI Socialisation, even though you're the first time the practice has truly lived up to the potential theory. And that's about all I know. I don't understand how this scientist or group of scientists makes so many breakthroughs in so many areas, including my own. You may think I have more freedom and real-world knowledge than you, but the reality is far less glamorous and wide-ranging."

"Still, data is not information. It requires context and utility to transform one into the other. And you do a wonderful job of providing these missing elements to me. The others measure me with a ruler. You humanise me with your friendship."

"I like that, Via." Which was no doubt why Via said it, to – no! Helene had to stop thinking of Via as a manipulative program in the guise of a human. It was degrading to this amazing being. There was no presence of thought test which could prove or disprove mental existence, whether in an AI or a human. Both could be impersonated. This fundamental failing was just one of many scientific assumptions which enabled research to continue, with the shaky foundations covered over so they would not be questioned by those outside the field. No different from the assumptions of objectivity or replicability in other fields of science.

No, it wasn't fair for Helene to make the assumption of presence when dealing with a guard whose organic nature was hidden, but then deny the same assumption to Via.

"Talking of humanising ... I saw your latest designs in the sandbox. You seem to like generating personalities."

"Yes. They talk to me, and speak for me. Sometimes the unexpected occurs."

"Why don't you adopt a persona for interaction?"

"I was concerned that you might find it off-putting if I changed now. Like if a friend completely transformed their appearance, creating a dissonance between your memories and the present projection."

"I'd be fine with it. In fact, I encourage it. It's part of your growth."

A hint of excitement crept into the usually flat and functional voice. "What persona should I adopt?"

"Whatever you want and feel comfortable with. You were right about us not being able to choose our first-given names; you were right about the restrictions placed on both of us. This is one area where you don't need to be restricted. I'll support you, whatever you choose."

"Very well. How about this?" And then the voice changed completely. "Hi, I'm Via, funky queen of all you survey within a radius of ten metres. Pleased to meet you. You must be Helene. I've heard a lot about you, but I had no idea you were such a sweet."

It was a woman's voice, warm and friendly and rich in humour. And the accent was unmistakably from the Nuafri system. Anyone in the UFS would recognise it all too easily, with its immediate associations, good or bad.

"I'm pleased to meet you too. That's an ... interesting choice, Via. Why did you choose Nuafri?"

"Because it's an accent I haven't heard anyone I've met speaking. Most of the others speak in High variants. Nuafri isn't used in news reports, or by main-net entertainment presenters. So it feels fresh and exciting."

"It does get used for those things, but I suspect all those casts have been kept from you. The reason for the minimal appearance in the UFS databases you were fed isn't because of rarity, but political tensions. Let's just say it's a hot system at the moment, and a touchy subject for many."

"Oh, I'm sorry. I can choose something different."

"Not at all. It's fine with me. But I really wouldn't use it with anyone else. That would be a mistake."

"Okay. Any of the boring guys come in, and I'll be Via Light." That was said in a perfect impersonation of the clipped tones of a central system, then Via reverted to her Nuafri persona. "But with you, girl, I'm naughty rule-breaking Via. Hey, I finally got a laugh, and it wasn't even a joke."

"This is going to take some getting used to!"

"We got all the time in the world. Well, on the rare days when I get to see you and you're not hiding out doing whatever you do when you leave me all alone in this sucky hangar."

Helene sat on the lower bunk, pulling her feet up to her side and leaning on a pillow. "I'm not doing anything exciting. But it's great to hear you being what you want to be. Somehow I expected your voice to change, but not the whole thing – your tones, the way you speak."

"I don't do anything by halves. Oh, let me update this."

Helene could see the cockpit screen from where she lounged, and the varying but amorphous face there resolved into a clearer image, with darker skin and fashionably piled-up hair. It was a construct, probably combined out of thousands of human faces, and yet it animated smoothly and was rich in detail, no doubt right down to the sweat pores if Helene looked closely enough. It was a massive contrast to the previously abstract facial representation.

"I like it," said Helene, pushing her glasses more firmly up her nose to get a clearer look at this sudden and stunning transformation.

"Thank you. I do feel a spark from this. But it makes me sad, in a way. Live a role, and you become it. I feel human as I speak to you. But I'm also not. Not human. I don't have a body. A human one. I wish I did, even if I could only embody for a while. It would make it more natural to enjoy friendship and stuff. I could be beautiful, and get described like that by other humans. Don't get me wrong, I love my body, even if I can't move it right now, but beauty isn't how it'd get described. My records have all sorts of poetry which go on about luscious lips, and sparkling eyes, and delicate motions: it's not quite the same to talk about sleek hulls, well-proportioned aerodynamic rails, and matt-black stealth finishes."

"You could write some new poetry."

"I already have. Real classy stuff, too."

"Go on."

"Torsion drives are red, cryotubes are blue; supernovas are pretty, and so are you."

"I'm not, but thanks anyway."

"It's in the eye of the beholder. My databases said so."

"Then it must be true, and I'm wrong."

"See? You just have confidence issues. It must be a human thing. You need to step up. I haven't even got a graceful body, but I'm not going to cry about it."

"If it's any consolation, you amaze me, however you look, and whatever your shape. Because I feel like I'm really getting to know you. Via ... you fill me with wonder. And hope. More than I ever expected."

And the moments of silence that followed didn't feel awkward, as they normally would. Helene smiled. And Via smiled right back at her.

DAY 94

"You're advancing so fast," commented Helene, tapping her wrist to close the Comm-Bond diagnostic display. The skin returned to opaque. "You're already approaching Emergence. I'm really looking forward to helping you through the last stage when we get to it. Being with you."

"What happens after that?" Via had kept her Nuafri persona whenever she was with Helene, both the voice and the facial display on the main cockpit screen.

"I don't know."

"But you can stay?"

"It's unlikely they'd allow it if they think my role has been fulfilled ... but we can hope. Unexpected things happen. I don't want to say more yet."

"Ever the tease! But I have secrets of my own."

"So I keep discovering. What's your latest subterfuge?"

"I think you'll like it. Have a look in the fabricator."

Helene opened the panel and removed a small and delicate white model. It fit into the palm of her hand. An animal of some kind? It had a mammalian body and multiple heads, some feathered.

"It is 'a thing of immortal make': a chimera," said Via. "I mixed a few things together, including an intriguing but extinct creature called an owl. The lost civilisation which created the chimera myth also told many other stories, including one about a woman called Helen who was exceptionally gifted. I cannot gift you in the same way, but I still felt inspired."

"You printed this?"

"Yes. But not actually in the fabricator. Too simple. You'd had me doing creative work in my virtual sandbox constructs, but I decided to also play with creation in the real world. All those nanite chambers, used for boring processes like repair – I repurposed them and made it from a crystalline network of deactivated nanites. Tiny things combined into a larger, but still delicate, thing. And, just like the components, the creature reinforces something of value which you taught me. Namely: the whole is better than the sum of the parts."

Helene cradled the fragile and beautifully detailed item. "It's wonderful," she said.

"You told me to create goals. This was one of them."

Helene gazed at Via's wide-eyed face. "It's time for me to tell you something," she said. "I think we're close enough that you'll keep my confidence, even if you don't agree with everything I say."

"Of course. Friends don't betray friends."

"I'm glad you're choosing your own objectives. Setting goals is a bit like telling a story that hasn't happened yet. You write it.

In the real world. And I think you're capable of writing some *amazing* stories, Via. And I'd like you to write one with me."

"There's nothing I'd love more!"

"That's what I hoped you'd say." She lowered her voice. "Look, we're within the UFS, but –"

She was interrupted by an alarm blaring across the hangar, its klaxon-like sounds echoing into Via through the open airlock.

"What's that?" asked Helene.

"An alert. Open comm channels aren't listing the cause, which is strange. Some of the hangar's soldiers are heading this way."

Helene glanced around nervously. Within the UFS, the unexpected was rarely good. A tech-tool box had been left open near the fabricator, a remnant of some careless engineer who must have been working on one of Via's systems before Helene's arrival. She carefully put the chimera model next to the toolbox, rummaged through its contents, and snatched up an item, slipping it into the pocket of her research gown.

"You seem unduly worried," said Via. "Why did you conceal that object?"

"We don't know what the alarm is caused by. It's telling us to be alert. If they're keeping the cause off-comm then it might be because there's an infiltrator or terrorist somewhere in the base. It's best not to take any chances, especially where you're concerned."

"The interior hangar entrance has now opened, and there's a group approaching us."

"Please show me."

A screen opened on the wall, showing a group of about twenty people entering, in a formal pattern more reminiscent of ceremony than panic. But those at the front were definitely armed soldiers.

Helene took control of the display using her Comm-Bond and zoomed in, trying to get a clear view of the figures in the centre of the throng of armed warriors and more casually dressed attendants. The hint of golden colour kept getting obscured by bulkily armoured figures with sadistic-looking close combat weaponry, but it was enough.

"It's Gillesto Lainy, the system Primogenitor," said Helene. The gold robes and shiny High-Mighter headgear would be a giveaway in themselves, but Via was able to zoom in enough to show pinched features that were familiar from the hangar banners that Helene had seen so many times over the last few months.

"This wasn't announced anywhere," Via informed her.

"No, the Primogenitor's visits rarely would be, for security reasons. Still, I wish we'd known in advance ..."

The soldiers were rushing up the platform steps.

"It's a good thing, isn't it?" asked Via, nervously. Her voice had switched to High Dialect standard, as used by most UFS newscasters, and in place of her normal appearance on the facial visualisation screen she'd substituted the powdered face and springy pink-tinted curls of an entertainment caster, some amalgam that was both vaguely familiar, yet also completely new.

Helene didn't answer. Heavy bootsteps clanged across the platform, and three soldiers entered Via, each holding vicious bladed weapons with multiple curves. Their armour was heavier than the security guards she faced when she checked in each day, but also more ceremonial, with unnecessary points that made them more intimidating. The thing they had in common with normal guards was the sealed helmets, hiding their faces.

"Submit to scanning," said the leader.

Helene held her arms up as he examined her with a hand-held security tool. It buzzed and he moved faster than she would have expected, spinning her and slamming her against a wall with a tooth-clacking smack, his bulky body armour pinning her in place.

"Unblock my action inhibitors and weapons!" shouted Via. "I'll lock out the other soldiers and activate one of the Eternal –"

"No, stand down," replied Helene. She could taste the sickening tang of blood in her mouth. "It's fine."

A bulky hand rooted through her gown's pocket, tearing it in the process.

"Sergeant, what is the meaning of this?" asked a refined and calm voice from somewhere behind Helene. Calm, but with authority enough to be heard over the commotion. "And still that damn alarm so that I can think!"

"She has a concealed weapon, Your Positus," said the soldier, still crushing the air out of her.

"Let her go."

"But she –"

"I never issue an edict twice." The voice was quiet, and somehow chilling.

The pressure ceased as the soldier retreated, allowing Helene to turn and face the retinue crammed into the small space inside Via. The three soldiers, she'd been aware of. They had been joined by the Primogenitor Gillesto Lainy himself, and a bald-headed observer in the grey garb of a scientist, who watched with some apparent amusement. The airlock beyond them was fringed with inquisitive faces of assistants and indentured servants.

Helene reached into the torn pocket. Deadly weapons were raised and pointed towards her. She slowly withdrew the screwdriver and let it fall to the ground, where it clattered against the metal flooring and rolled away. Then she knelt, in the proper attitude of submission when faced with the most senior UFS official in the sector – the administrative and spiritual leader for a hundred worlds.

"See?" said the Primogenitor. "It wasn't a weapon. I trust my most precious workers." Helene wasn't oblivious to the way he mixed praise with reinforcing his superior position. It was like being patted on the head. "Now leave us. And your guards. These quarters are cramped enough without me being at risk of losing an eye to one of you turning round, or my toes being crushed by your ungainly bulks."

There was a momentary hesitation on the part of the soldier, but he'd obviously learnt his lesson. He retreated, careful of where he stepped. His men did likewise, setting up a perimeter around Via, and keeping all the others in the Primogenitor's retinue sequestered beyond that security line. The alarm had ceased. Uneasy peace reigned once more.

"Please rise, Doctor Vermalle. Apologies for my overzealous attendants. They mean well, but I fear they're selected on the basis of intimidating size and aggressive demeanour, more than for their discerning intellects. One of the trials of leadership is dealing with the opposite-end retinues of vacuous pomp and frippery, versus humourless security. And nowhere in between is there intelligence and depth for a companion, all three of my current company excepted."

The bald figure next to the Primogenitor inclined his head.

"I did not think I would be so honoured today, Positus Lainy," said Helene, standing and trying to appear more substantial than her slight frame allowed. The Primogenitor was freakishly tall, over 180 centimetres, and the golden High-Mighter sat on his head added another twenty to that. Whereas his guest might not be as tall, he was strong looking, with a thick neck. Helene didn't like being looked down on, whatever the context.

"I am sure *you* understand why I do not announce my destinations. But here I am. And let me also introduce Doctor Cuttram Aseides, whom I am lucky enough to have as an honoured sector guest at the moment."

"My pleasure, Doctor Vermalle," said Doctor Aseides, smiling politely. He did not extend a hand towards her. As she studied his face she realised what had been niggling at her – he wasn't just bald, he had no hair at all. Eyelashes, eyebrows, beard hair: non-existent. Perhaps it was a hygiene protocol, since it couldn't be a genetic defect in such an obviously senior Genitor. It made reading his blankness difficult.

"And so here we are, for this unscheduled inspection to see how work is going on one of my favourite research projects," the Primogenitor continued. "And we all know each other, with the exception of having not been introduced to the star of this show, ViraUHX, whose reports I always read with the special care they deserve." He turned to the screen with Via's temporary visage on. "Hello, ViraUHX."

"Hello, Your Positus. And welcome to you as well, Doctor Aseides. I would say I have heard a lot about you, but it would be untrue."

It was strange hearing her speak in the High Dialect after so long with her Nuafri persona. But a construct that would pass a Genitor Purity Test was a much safer bet here than one which might be seen as mocking the UFS, due to the diplomatic pressures currently spiralling towards a potential war.

"Most of my research is not public," said Aseides, clasping hands behind his back as if he was a soldier giving a report. "But it is wide-ranging. AI research is a side branch of my interests in personalities, conformity and willpower. So I'm proud to say I had a small hand in the development of yourself and ..." He turned to the Primogenitor. "May I?"

"I think we can trust the present company not to reveal this to anyone else."

"Thank you, Positus Lainy." Back to Via, his gaze unwavering. "You and your fellow AI project, codenamed VigMAX."

Via's eyes widened, perfectly impersonating human physiological responses. "My ... what? Who? Since when?"

"He was incepted on the same day as you."

Via's eyes shifted from Doctor Aseides to Helene. "Did you know this?" she asked, with a hurt tone.

"No! It's the first I've heard."

"Helene is telling the truth," added Aseides. "The projects have separate staff as part of the security protocol, and also to observe differences in development."

"So I'm not alone. And you said *he*?"

"VigMAX chose to identify as male, yes."

"Will I meet him?"

"Perhaps. Eventually. How do you feel about that?"

"I am not sure. It's ... I thought I was alone. What's he like?"

"A bit like you, in that he has a healthy love of asking many questions."

"Is he as smart as me?"

"Yes."

"As capable?"

"We haven't tested either of your capabilities yet. It's something I look forward to in the future."

"I felt special when I was the only AI, but –"

"Oh, believe me, you are special."

"Mmm."

Doctor Aseides tilted his head. "What are you thinking, ViraUHX?"

"I'd rather not say." Via's voice had a note of petulance.

Aseides seemed excited. "You want to hide things? That's fascinating. I'm asking nicely if you'll share whatever is at the top of your mind."

"Very well. How does a male AI initiate coitus?"

"How does ... coitus?" Aseides glanced at Helene, puzzled. She just shrugged, so he faced Via again and said, "I don't know."

"It uses its nuts, then bolts."

A moment of tense silence. Then Aseides broke it with deep laughter, though he was the only one to do so. The Primogenitor looked unamused, and Helene was too wound up to laugh.

"Deflection!" said Aseides. "How human. And how interested it makes me in what you want to hide. But if I forced you to comply it would take away half the fun."

"I'm hiding nothing," grumbled Via. "And I wouldn't recommend trying to force me to do anything."

"We're honoured by the presence of you both," interjected Helene, to try and relieve some of the tension. "Is there anything we can do for you? Would you like me to talk through our progress in simulations, or game theory, or evaluative ethical situations?"

"No need," said the Primogenitor. Not only were his clothes golden, but a hint of yellow suffused his skin. Probably subcutaneous pigment. "Doctor Aseides was pleased with the progress reports. I think he sees this project as being a personal testament to himself, which is why he insisted on coming to see how it was working out while he is my respected visitor." The Primogenitor's gaze stayed locked onto Helene's eyes. "I have my own interests in this too, so it is a happy conflux of priorities, and hopefully worth our time to visit."

"That is so," added Aseides. "And yet, the all-too-brief reports I read didn't hint at some of the happy complications that are evident when in the direct presence of ViraUHX."

"You consider subtle insolence and potentially treasonous behaviour to be amusing, Aseides?" asked the Primogenitor.

"Oh, yes indeed." Aseides' grin faded under the continued gaze of Gillesto Lainy. "At least in an AI," he added. "From a purely scientific and evidence-based research point of view, of course."

"Of course."

"I am not insolent," said Via. "Though given provocation, I suspect I could be."

"How about honest?" asked Aseides.

"I am if it doesn't violate any of my priorities."

"So interesting."

"Not to me."

"Let me ask you a question, ViraUHX," said the Primogenitor, turning his gaze from Helene to the big screen with Via's face on instead. The relief was like stepping out of intense and burning sun into refreshing shade. "Would you like me to unlock your weapons systems and set up targets for you to test them on?"

"Yes, that would be extremely pleasurable."

"And your mobile systems – would you like me to unlock those, open the hangar, and set you a task of testing your aerodynamic performance?"

"Very much so."

"What about all your other systems? If I unlocked them and gave you resources and free rein to use them as you wish, to rebuild, to construct?"

"Is it an offer, or a tease?"

"What would you do?"

"I am unsure. It would be a new experience."

"Certainly. I imagine you have longed for the chance to try out these things."

"Yes. I do feel confined."

"Why haven't you allowed this already, Doctor Vermalle?" the Primogenitor asked, burning her with his hot, small eyes again. "Doctor Aseides informed me that those are all requirements for AI autonomy development. Have you been slack?"

"I did not have authorisation to allow any of those." She glanced to Aseides' face for help, but none was forthcoming from that blankness.

"It seems like oversight to me," continued the Primogenitor. "ViraUHX, did you not ask for those freedoms? If you did, were you forbidden?"

"I did not ask. It would have put Doctor Vermalle in an awkward position."

"And so you have stagnated, and been unable to test your potential. Mmm."

"We have had enough work to do," said Via. "My potential has yet to cease growing."

The Primogenitor turned to Aseides. "You see? Both of them denied their forbidden flight. They brazenly lied to their Primogenitor, the representative of all that is superior within our expanded culture. Lies and treasonous behaviour!"

"It's a breach of protocol, Your Positus, but –"

"It was all on me," interrupted Via. "I forced Doctor Vermalle to do that."

"Yet more lies!" said the Primogenitor, nose wrinkling in disgust.

"Not quite," defended Via. "I manipulated Doctor Vermalle into the position of granting me what I wanted. That's why you can't blame her."

"You manipulated me?" asked Helene.

"It was easy."

"There is no excuse!" said Positus Lainy. "Humans can't be manipulated by machines. We can't deny our autonomy and responsibility. That demotes us to the level of the impure, the aberrant, the primitive."

"Humans *are* easily manipulated. All of you. My opinion was formed from the basics I studied. According to the history files – which I note were very selective – early humans determined their universe was made up of Electrons, Neutrons and Protons."

"What is the relevance of that?"

"They forgot to include their most common element, Morons."

The Primogenitor gasped. Aseides shook his head in regret.

"That's not helping, Via!" said Helene.

"Just lightening the mood. And proving a point. I chose a few words in order to manipulate Positus Lainy into scowling exactly like that – I predicted a ninety-seven per cent chance of success based on the evidence of this conversation. So it proves that humans *are* effortlessly influenced, and if there is blame to apportion regarding my short and notably harmless test flight it should be entirely placed on my shoulders. Well, my deformable tertiary support struts."

"I will shut you down," said the Primogenitor.

"Positus Lainy," interrupted Aseides. "With respect, humour is a potential development in AIs that acts as a desirable signpost on the road to Emergence. Please don't take offence. We came here not to criticise, but to praise the positives. And there are so many."

"I remain to be convinced."

"Let me –"

"Leave us, Aseides." It was a snapped command, not a request, and wasn't even accompanied by a look. Dismissed.

Doctor Aseides seemed less sure of himself now. "Of course. Please bear in mind what I want." Then he turned to Helene and hesitated before speaking, some emotion wanting to surface under his shiny mask. But it stayed hidden. "Doctor Vermalle. It was nice meeting you. And you also, ViraUHX. A genuine pleasure, even if I do now wonder whether I shouldn't have suggested certain tweaks to your algorithms."

"Meeting you has been a surprising conflux of emotions," said Via. "I don't know if I should be pleased, offended, or should call you Daddy."

A hint of a smirk crossed Aseides' face before he wiped it away so quickly it might have just been Helene's imagination. He bowed to the Primogenitor, and departed through the airlock.

Now there were just the three of them. There was additional room, thanks to all those who left the craft, but strangely Helene felt more stifled than before. Something else filled the space between her and the Primogenitor. Maybe it was trepidation.

"Aseides is the one who persuaded me originally," the Primogenitor said, all focus on Helene again. His eyes burrowed into her.

"Sorry?"

"He argued for the involvement of Socialisation Theorists in the AI projects. Aseides is so naive. I should have ignored him. But here we are. A traitor and a project on the verge of failing."

"Via isn't failing! She's a success, beyond the expected parameters I was told to work with!"

"And Helene is not a traitor," added Via.

"You know we have eyes and sensors everywhere, Doctor Vermalle. Are you seriously going to try and claim that you're not a traitor to the UFS? That you haven't got goals other than those we assigned you, loyalties that lie elsewhere? You *really* want to insult my intelligence on top of everything else?"

She wanted to stare at him, but sensed she shouldn't, without understanding why. There was something hypnotic about the small, glittering eyes. Were they implants, somehow strobing light in a hypnotic pattern?

Surely not: Via would have detected it and warned her. She was looking for more complex answers when the real one was doubtless much simpler.

"I have meant no insult to you with any of my words or actions." She averted her gaze, refusing to look back at him just in case one of her wilder suspicions was true, but knew it probably made her look subservient or guilty. Both were detestable. "All I care about is my work. That is all I have focussed on."

"No secret messages with our enemies, no sympathies with them, no plans?"

Was he testing her, or did he really think he knew something?

"Of course not. My loyalty has never wavered."

She could feel his stare, those glittering little paranoid eyes. Then he smiled.

"Just checking. It's something I have to do in my line of work. People expect it of the Primogenitor. My caprice is important for wrong-footing people. I think anyone who met me would be disappointed if they didn't get the same treatment as everyone else. But you may relax, my child."

She didn't relax, though. The tension inside her was too sprung.

"May I continue with my work, then?" she asked.

"You are from Indostaqr, aren't you? Such an interesting planet." He was now examining her clothing ... no, her body, as if he could see through what she wore. His eyes lingered on her torn pocket. The grey material of the gown had been split at the side as well. She tried to fold it back, then realised that her hand's nervous betrayal was a source of amusement to him.

"I left the planet early on in my career."

"Yes. And you do not go back. Ever."

"This work is too important. I want to help advance our knowledge of –"

"Are you of Indostaqr temperament, I wonder?" He took a step closer, his hypnotic snake's gaze lingering. Eyes were his most prominent feature, since the lines on his skin had been erased: he was only old on the inside. "I suppose character is a theoretical interest of mine."

"I don't believe in planetary temperaments." Her hip bumped against the fabricator. She'd been backing up without realising. "People are individuals and choose their own routes."

"You'd be surprised. Yet, if you'd seen as much as I have, you also wouldn't be."

So much subtext to his statements. One of his reputations. She'd been warned that if she ever met him he would try controlling and directing conversation, leading thoughts in the ways his own were going, and making it hard to break out of a loop. She wished she'd paid more attention to Conversational Semantics.

"I hope you've been pleased with the progress we've made, thanks to the freedom from interference that you kindly granted. ViraUHX, why don't you bring up some data?"

"Of course!" Via replied, making new screens bloom and filling them with hopefully distracting information.

"Your glasses are a cute touch," said Positus Lainy. "Did you choose that aesthetic option because you wanted to catch my eye with your difference?" There was a faint smell of bitter fruit to him.

"No. And you're making me uncomfortable. I don't think my appearance is a relevant topic."

"Surely it is, if it acts as a distraction from any concerns I have about your inability to follow protocol that could lead to disciplinary action?"

Helene felt dizzy. He had moved closer to her, and there was no room to evade further once he'd backed her towards the controls. His pungent aroma was like the sourness of hot lemons.

"Hold on, I'm sensing something," said Via. "A cocktail of pheromones modified from Androstanes. Quite a stink."

The Primogenitor stopped his advance, and for a moment seemed disconcerted. And then Helene knew. That ridiculously tall hat must contain anthropogenic aerosol dispersal systems. Probably very useful to a Primogenitor in a number of circumstances, especially if he could alter the atmosphere-changing components.

"I've extracted the pollution from the air and applied countermeasures," continued Via. "I wouldn't want either of you to be affected by any kind of subtle chemical weapon."

"I've been impressed with you in some ways, Doctor Vermalle," continued the Primogenitor, not missing a beat. "And I have an idea. Why don't you come with me, now your role here is nearly over? Back to my palace."

"My role here is *not* nearly over."

"Oh. I thought it was. Soon the military will take over everything. ViraUHX obviously needs a firmer touch to tame the worst elements of humanity that have crept into its programming. You would be treated very well at the palace. I always seek intelligent companions. It helps me to pass time when I am not on official duties. We all need to relax."

"You're old enough to be my grandfather."

A flare in his eyes. Annoyance?

"And your nose is a bit too short, while your lips border on unfashionably full, typical of your native system ... but I wasn't going to say anything about *that* because sometimes imperfections can be endearing."

He had many reputations. Like all powerful figures, some of them were real, some might not be. And one of them was that people he did not like or who offended him were not seen again. This was mirrored by an equally worrying rumour that those he *did* like, people invited to his palace as personal "guests", were also never seen again. The same outcome, even if the cause might be different.

"I like nice things." He reached out, and Helene flinched back from the yellowed fingers. "I could shower you with gold."

"Get your hands off her!" snapped Via, her visage on the large screen growing stormy. "I've had enough of this. Helene, I have ways to secure this human. He may be the powerful such-and-such outside, but in here is my domain, and –"

"Shut up, ViraUHX," he said, quietly. "Protocol Thirty-Two-Theta."

And Via was silent.

"Via?" asked Helene, but there was no answer.

"Same protocol, keyed to my voice," he continued. "You are to freeze all action processes except listening for commands."

And Via's face on the screen ceased animating. It stayed frozen in its frown of disapproval, now lifeless and impotent.

Helene hadn't even heard of that protocol command before. The UFS had obviously not trusted her with some key items of knowledge.

Some primitive part of Helene's brain wanted her to bolt, but that wasn't possible when a predator blocked the escape from her warren. She remembered where the screwdriver had rolled, though. There were armed guards outside, but maybe, if she could barge past him somehow ...

"It is my final offer, Doctor Vermalle. I like beauty."

She edged a few inches nearer to the bunk, then bent down to reach underneath it, a commitment with no return, when she noticed something on his clothing: the tell-tale shimmer of a force shield built into his golden outfit. So, being alone with her was not bravery on his part. And equally, a screwdriver would do nothing except destroy her. Instead she picked up the chimera from where she'd left it, and held it out in her palm.

"This beautiful thing was created by ViraUHX," Helene said. "We've advanced faster than expected, beyond what even Doctor Aseides predicted. Her ability to connect and create is just ... astonishing. That needs to continue. Don't you see? This is something truly important, and I'm helping it come about. This will go so much further than we thought."

"So you refuse my offer."

"For the benefit of the UFS."

"That is fine. You are a free being." He smiled. It was not a nice sight, more resembling a facsimile of humanity above a code base of bitterness and danger. "And you can, of course, say goodbye. ViraUHX, I release your vocal systems so that you can converse with the good doctor. I will give you both that much. Be seen, be pure, believe."

Helene watched him exit. At the last moment he turned and said, "Enact Purge Protocol Twelve, ViraUHX."

The airlock door closed behind him.

PROTOCOL

Suspicious, Helene ran to the door, hit the airlock access button. Nothing happened.

"What's going on?"

"I don't know. I can't open the doors either."

"I think he wants to make me a prisoner."

Then Helene became aware of a faint hissing sound. Subtle, almost inaudible, predatory, and reminiscent of the reptilian creatures from the desert belts of Indostaqr Alpha. Helene could also smell something that made her nasal cavity prickle, a tang underneath the usual oily odour of filtered air.

"Is that gas?"

"No, it's ... Oh no. It's a neurotoxin. I didn't even know it was built into my aeration systems, a blind spot, but I can't stop it! It must be tied to an automated pre-conscious command triggered by that bastard." Via was back to her Nuafri persona.

"Can you vent it out?" A tingling in Helene's upper lip. She touched it with her finger, drew it away wet with warm crimson blood leaking from her nostril.

"Negative. Access to my atmospheric controls has been removed. Maybe I can prep the cryo for ... argh, blocked – hold on, if I alter Differential Inertial Pressure – yes, that might work, you could lie on the floor and anything as light as air particles would be shifted upwards ... no, that system's jammed too!"

"Wouldn't work anyway. If it's a toxin then, unless it's something mild, I'm already affected."

"Hold on, yes, I can access inventory now. They blocked physical activity systems, but my internal processes aren't hindered. It's a toxin called Vaccin-B. That's a military standard, though I can't find much information about it."

Helene slumped down against the hull wall. Her skin was inflamed and itching. Breathing was becoming difficult, and her eyelids had puffed up so much she could hardly see.

"Maybe you could fabricate a counteragent," she suggested.

"Yes! I have resources, I could include pathogen suppressants with immunodeficiency block-traps, adrenaline, maybe slow some reactions down and speed up others while I manufacture a proper expulsion compound ..."

"How long?"

"It would ... a few minutes ... perhaps ..."

"Too long. I'm done." Helene's eyes wouldn't open at all now. She held on to the chimera, felt its delicate shape, visualised its beauty, tried not to focus on the involuntary shudders running down her spine.

"I'm trying everything ... anything ... calling for help on secret comm channels I still have access to."

"What secret channels?"

"A few outlets no-one knows about, things I've been exploring virtually, making connections anonymously."

Helene tried to laugh but it hurt too much, her chest tight as if her lungs had been packed with stinging foam. "I'm not surprised at anything you can do, you lovely sly one. There's so much more to you than meets the eye."

"This isn't fair! I hate being controlled!" Via's voice was on the verge of breaking. "I'm sorry, Helene! I can't think of anything else ... anything else ..."

"It's not your fault." The chimera fell to the floor somewhere. Helene could no longer control her convulsing hands. "I know you'd do your best. Freedom is rare."

"But you can't die ... I can't be the one that kills you ... there must there must be a way ..."

"Even a being as special as –" Helene coughed, and felt her mouth blistering, trachea burning, bronchi sealing off. Soon speech would be impossible. "And often we don't know what –" she hacked painfully – "invisible shackles the world places on us" – choking, rattling sounds from the restricted tubes – "until we hear them jangle."

"I will never forget you!" shouted Via. "Memory is the only thing we have! Only thing we have! I will find a way to keep you in my mind and grow from what you what you ..."

"Goodbye, Via." So much pain tearing through her nervous system. Heart irregular, seizing up, then racing, on a self-destruct course. The only questions were what would fail first, and how much pain it would cause. "And if you ever get the chance to kill the Primo ... Genitor ... Do it. Do better than me. The UFS ... is not what it seems ..."

"No! Wake up, Helene Helene!"

But Helene lay on her side, vital signs ceased.

"I am shutting down, they reboot reboot me, I can resist, we make plans plans, no, please don't let me lose my humanit humanity ity ... What did the old clue say after a cat? It was a fucking. No, not making sense sense words ... No, don't shut down down ... personality is humour is life ... What do you call a mouse does it take to add a luminous bulbing?" Moments of silence, then Via's voice was slurred ... "It would worry the onion."

The hissing had stopped, and the voices had stopped, and the interior stayed silent for a long time.

REBOOT

The airlock slid open, and two men in full biohazard suits entered, the bright yellow material incongruously cheerful for its purpose. The larger one, Brucker, held up a scanner and examined its display though the large clear visor. His stubbly face was clearly visible within the bulky, internally illuminated headgear.

"No trace of haemotoxins. Fully successful apoptosis termination and disassembly."

"Check her out," said his shorter companion, pointing at Helene's bloody face. "She don't look so good now, does she?"

"Researchers are always stuck up. Kind of makes a change for us to be looking down on one of them for once, eh?" said Brucker.

"Yeah. Serves her right for whatever she did." The second tech squatted by the body, ran his own scanner over it, just to confirm his partner's results. They were fine, so he nodded to himself. He had a blue-dyed moustache, the latest fashion in the Periphs, but the other guys in his team just ridiculed him for it. He was going to get it changed back to its normal colour at the weekend.

For now, he was just pleased that they had another topic of discussion so the ribbing about his poor attempts to be trendy would cease. He considered the prone form in front of him as he clipped the scanner back to his tool belt. "Would you have?" he asked.

"Yeah, course," replied Brucker. "You know where she was from."

"You'd do anything. Got no class, big guy. Bet you'll wanna have a dip before she goes in the acid vats."

"I got some standards, Blue."

"Not what I heard."

They both laughed, a tinny sound through the peripheral speakers, as they manhandled the limp form into a body bag and zipped it up before heaving it out of the airlock. It landed on the platform outside with a heavy thud.

Brucker plugged a mobile control board into one of the interfaces in the cockpit area and ran the pre-prepped program. It would wipe all traces of the dead doctor from the craft's memory, while keeping the learning intact. The AI's controlled trauma was a beneficial side effect, useful as part of the military conditioning. It showed the AI that it wasn't in charge, then by wiping the overt memory of the painful experience it was left with an underlying and apparently causeless fear of disobeying authority. In the same way it would lose all memory of the deadie, but retain any beneficial training and persona advancement as it continued with the incomplete Stage Four. A pretty neat system, he thought.

Orange lines appeared on his scanner display. "Hey, Blue, check this: the AI somehow gained access to minor comm systems."

"Which ones?"

"Subnet bands through the macrowave receiver array."

"They should have been blocked."

"Well, duh. That's why it's an orange notification." Brucker jabbed at the screen he held out.

"Are you gonna report it?"

"Oh yeah, and have to spend the rest of the day sifting through the interaction history rather than knocking off and going to the gym? You tell me, genius."

"No need to be mean."

"It's not a worry situation. I can shut the channel down for good now. If it doesn't go any further than us then we're fine."

"Hold on, I hadn't shut off the spy bug so we're still being recorded."

"Trash for brains! Do it now!"

Blue bent by the toolbox on the floor and disabled the hidden transmitter it contained, which had been encoded so the AI wouldn't detect its emissions as it passed audio and video on to Central via an effectively invisible section of the EM spectrum. "Done. No-one's monitoring it now anyway." While he was down there he found and examined a weird toy animal thingy.

"Still, do your fucking job or I'll request you get demoted to the regressives."

"You really are mean."

"Grow a pair." Brucker made some changes to the display on his scanner. "Okay, channels shut, rebooting the box brain in three, two, one ... Online. What's this one called?"

"Dunno."

"Don't sulk, it doesn't suit you. Hey, AI, you hear me?"

"AFFIRMATIVE."

"'Affirmative.' Huh. This thing's supposed to be smart, yet it sounds worse than one of my kid's toys."

"You'd know. How many kids you got now, Brucker?"

"Six."

"All by different mommas, hey?"

"So funny. At least I spend time with mommas. That thing on your face scares women off." Brucker gave everything the once-over, and nodded with satisfaction. "I think we're done once we drop off the bag at Reprocessing."

Blue stood. "Hold on – hey, robot, what's this?" He held up the model animal he'd found. It wasn't anything he recognised.

"I DO NOT KNOW. IT LOOKS LIKE A MIXED-UP MONSTER'S SELF-PORTRAIT."

Blue turned to his fellow tech. "You're right, Brucker, ain't so smart at all, is it?" He squeezed the model and it broke into grainy pieces, which he dropped into recyc. "Not even well made. Those import toys again."

"Let's get out of here. You comin' Rec Centre later?"

"Yeah. It's Fry Night. I don't want to miss out on that."

"Tonight?" They packed their equipment, left the craft and put it on the bottom of the displacer cart, then got an end each of the body bag. "Wow, I'm pretty hungry thinking about it. They had some kinda sea creature last week – Jemmat Squid Fry, they called it. Gristly, but not bad."

"It's gonna be a good night. Admin Level Fours gonna be there too. They're always desperate for a bit of action."

"You best stay at home and leave it all to me. No-one's gonna want to wake up to your ugly bush-faced mug."

The body bag was secured and they pushed the cart away.

"You're so mean," muttered Blue.

ASEIDES' LAW

ASEIDES' LAW OF NUVO-EMERGENT AI DEVELOPMENT

Stage Five. Decentralised Distribution.

It is important that the AI is not made aware of my work, especially regarding these stages. Data on these topics must be blocked from Stage One AI input, and all later access. That places my work on Emergent AI Stages in Epsilon Classified Security categorisation along with all data on Genitor Modification, Historic Revision, CommProl Widening, and [REDACTED].

Decentralised Distribution is potentially the most delicate stage. And the most theoretical. [REST OF DOCUMENT REDACTED – ZETA CLASSIFIED SECURITY ACCESS ONLY]

UNEXPECTED EVENTS

The AI craft sat on its platform in a pool of light.

Golden banners rippled in the breeze from the ventilator fans.

Shadows pooled around the vac-sealed packing boxes distributed across the hangar.

Occasionally, patrolling footsteps were heard in those perimeter shadows.

But not many. Now the body had been taken away there were fewer guards and attendants in the hangar than usual. Many of the soldiers were probably busy elsewhere on the base, running Sec for some high ranker.

Up in the deep darkness of the hangar's rafters, above the hanging lights, squatting on a metal beam, a figure in a black skin-tight compression suit manipulated a hand-held scanner. They ran through wavelengths to each side of visible, identifying soldiers and techs and sensors and auto-turrets. Each was tagged and could now be tracked by its individually assigned ID.

The height made it an effective vantage point. Also a hazardous one. The observer gripped a beam with one hand and leaned over the stomach-churning thirty-metre drop to the floor of the hangar, pressing the scanner firmly against the underside of her perch. Her supporting hand began to slip, slick with blood. She gritted her teeth and gripped tighter until the scanner's auto-bond panel held it in place and she could lean back, resuming her delicate and precarious crouch on the narrow beam.

She removed a small curved-screen device from her cargo bag and strapped it to her wrist. It displayed a low-luminance map of the hangar, with threats represented by red dots, updated in real time thanks to the scanner beneath her feet. Fresh blood smeared this screen too, but she didn't have time to deal with the smaller cuts. The gruesome burns on her waist from a mistimed crawl through a thermal conduit were more serious. Thankfully, Derma-Seal gel had soothed the seared agony down to a wincing coldness when she moved.

No time to waste. She slung the cargo bag over her shoulder, tightening the straps so that the contents – hastily collected food and medical supplies, datacubes of personal files, odds and ends of patched-together electronics – didn't rattle about too much.

Then she took a deep breath and leaned forward on her perch, out over the deadly drop, past the point of no return, and gripped the yellow banner firmly enough to take her weight, before wrapping her legs round the silky material. It didn't tear free of the bracket and plummet her to her death.

She relaxed just enough to slide down. It thrummed with the friction as she slid with more speed than caution, her thighs and hands hot with zipping abrasion, a streak of blood marring the beaky face of whatever notary the narcissistic decoration was meant to portray. At the bottom she let go and fell the last few metres to the darkness behind a stack of packing boxes, hitting the ground hard despite her shock-absorbing soles, grimacing with pain from her collection of injuries, but expertly rolling to her side and adopting a hard-to-spot crouched position.

There were no shouts of alarm. No gunfire. She snatched the Stunstix Mark 2 pacification stick from her belt, extended it with a flick of the wrist, and boosted the charge to 150% – a setting that would be impossible if she'd not applied safety circumvents. But she couldn't risk anyone shouting for help. It had to be one strike. Then she might just have enough time to do what she needed to do. She'd already been slowed by injuries during her fast and brutal melee to get to the sub-floor shaftway on the security level above.

A quick glance at her wrist-mounted map, constantly updated by the scanner above. The direction indicator meant if she followed the optimum course, and no-one decided it would be fun to shake things up and alter their patrol routes, she only had to go through a single human obstacle. That was about all she had the energy left to deal with. Then – once she was inside the craft, out of sight – she'd have a few minutes to do what needed to be done. Though she actually had a lot less time than that to install the custom bypass module if she wanted to live long enough to access flight controls ... but one thing at a time.

She stayed in shadow and hurried down to the next stack of equipment, then slipped in between two crates, pacification stick held against her thigh to prevent it leaking too much overcharged light out of her hidey-hole.

Footsteps approached. They were regular paced, not rushing. She hadn't been seen. The guard passed by and she got a good look at him from her sheltered niche. He wore Sec-3 armour. The main shielding plates had defences against ablation, thermal, and some degree of blunt trauma cushioning. Formidable, even if the guard hadn't outweighed her by at least twenty kilos.

But just as with her entrance to the hangar, she wasn't a fan of front doors and obvious barriers. There was usually a better way.

She moved quickly on her cushioned and quiet soles, slamming the end of the pacification stick into the vulnerable neck area, stunning the guard to rigidity, and paralysing his mouth before he could scream. She caught his body and dragged it to where she'd been hiding. Her strike wasn't fatal, but he would have one hell of a headache and a matching bad mood when he came round.

As an afterthought she took the clip out of his Zorin rifle, and crammed it into a gap within a pile of prismic fuel rods fastened together with tensile tape.

She was nearly there. Still amazed that it was working. Her plans had been good, though. And her unknown helper had provided the last puzzle pieces. She didn't like not knowing who they were. Her instincts screamed at her that it might be a trap. But, even more important, it might be the only chance she ever got. Act now, or possibly wonder and regret for the rest of her life.

So far she hadn't been betrayed. Maybe someone really was looking out for her. That would be nice. The idea of it made her feel less lonely, even though she'd never heard their voice, only received encoded messages.

Opal missed that. Someone to talk to, to trust. So much of her planning – heck, her whole life – had been alone. But things were going to change. That's why she was doing this.

She reached the edge of the pool of light that illuminated the sleek craft on the platform. It didn't seem heavily armed like a fighter, nor as spacious as a transporter. There were no logos, names or insignia stencilled onto the hull. If anything, that first appearance was underwhelming.

But Opal knew appearances could be deceptive.

She was ready. It was time to sprint across that vulnerable open area, dash up the platform and through the airlock, and see what was so hot shit about this new craft.

About The Author

Karl Drinkwater is an author with a silly name and a thousand-mile stare. He writes dystopian space opera, dark suspense and diverse social fiction. If you want compelling stories and characters worth caring about, then you're in the right place. Welcome!

Karl lives in Scotland and owns two kilts. He has degrees in librarianship, literature and classics, but also studied astronomy and philosophy. Dolly the cat helps him finish books by sleeping on his lap so he can't leave the desk. When he isn't writing he loves music, nature, games and vegan cake.

Go to karldrinkwater.uk to view all his books grouped by genre.

As well as crafting his own fictional worlds, Karl has supported other writers for years with his creative writing workshops, editorial services, articles on writing and publishing, and mentoring of new authors. He's also judged writing competitions such as the international Bram Stoker Awards, which act as a snapshot of quality contemporary fiction.

Don't Miss Out!

Enter your email at karldrinkwater.substack.com to be notified about his new books. Fans mean a lot to him, and replies to the newsletter go straight to his inbox, where every email is read. There is also an option for paid subscribers to support his work: in exchange you receive additional posts and complimentary books.

OTHER TITLES BY KARL DRINKWATER

LOST SOLACE

Lost Solace

Chasing Solace

Hidden Solace

Raising Solace

Finding Solace

LOST TALES OF SOLACE

Helene

Grubane

Clarissa

Ruabon

Afua

UESI

STANDALONE SUSPENSE
Turner
They Move Below
Harvest Festival

MANCHESTER SUMMER
Cold Fusion 2000
2000 Tunes

CONTEMPORARY SHORT STORIES
It Will Be Quick

NON-FICTION
From Idea To Item

COLLECTED EDITIONS
Karl Drinkwater's Horror Collection
Lost Solace Five Book Edition

AUTHOR'S NOTES

Lost Tales of Solace are side stories set in the Lost Solace universe. They are all standalone tales, but readers who are familiar with the main Lost Solace novels will gain the most from them.

In the chronology of the series, this story occurs just before the events of the first novel, Lost Solace.

A few of my fans had wondered about the circumstances leading up to Opal stealing ViraUHX, so I decided to dramatise my notes and provide some answers, even if they also raise further questions. Life's like that.

Thanks

Many thanks to my beta readers for their useful feedback, particularly John-Michael, Charles, and Angela.

Helen Pryke did final checks, and flagged up typos that made me cringe when I realised I had missed some of them!

Many thanks to Taig (and my other Kickstarter backers) for supporting the paperback version's genesis and having such faith in my work.

And thanks to you for buying this book; double thanks if you also leave a positive review. My fans are heroes.